The Christmas Mouse

Story by Toby Forward

Pictures by Ruth Brown

Sandy Creek
NEW YORK

When the wind snapped cold, and the icicles hung like sharks' teeth from the gutters, and the trees bent low in the wind, Tim snuffled round the skirting board, and rubbed his paws together and twitched his whiskers and wondered what Christmas would bring him this year.

When the pine trees towered in the corner of the
rooms, and the scent of forests filled the air, and the logs crackled
in the grates, and the hangings cast colored shadows on the carpets,
Ben rubbed his paws together and smoothed his whiskers and sniffed
the good things that were being made for Christmas.

On Christmas Eve, behind the wall, in the dark tunnels where the cats could not stalk and the dogs could not run, Tim stood in the secret place where mice can scurry. Ben came toward him dragging a fat, juicy, candied plum.

"Merry Christmas, Ben," said Tim. He held out a box, tied with a red ribbon end. Ben sucked in his cheeks. "I don't care about Christmas," he said. "It's all the same to me, whatever day it is."

"That looks like a nice plum," said Tim, hopefully.

"Yes. It is," said Ben, and he dragged the fat plum down the tunnel between the walls, and Tim looked at the box tied with the red ribbon end.

Back in his room, Tim tucked himself into his bed and sighed.

"It's all the same to me, as well," he said. And he blew out the light.

Ben snuggled down into his bed, and sighed.

"Christmas," he said to himself. "It's just another day."

While Tim curled up and slept soundly, Ben wriggled and turned.

"Can't you sleep?" asked a small voice.

"Who's there?" asked Ben.

"Just a friend." A tiny mouse peered through the frosty edge of Ben's window.

"Go away," said Ben.

"Don't you want some company? It's nearly Christmas."

"Christmas," said Ben. "Huh! It's all the same to me."

"Then go to sleep."

"I can't," said Ben.

"Then you might as well talk to me – seeing as you're awake anyway."

"All right then. Come on in," said Ben.

The little mouse pushed open the window
and scrambled through. He was thin and cold.
"Brr," he said. He went and stood by the dying
embers of Ben's fire. "That's better."

"Careful," said Ben. "You're blocking the heat
from me."

"Sorry, Ben."

"How do you know my name?" asked Ben.
"And who are you?"

"Jake," said the mouse. But he did not answer
Ben's other question. "That's a nice plum," he said.

"It's mine," said Ben. "For Christmas."
He jumped out of bed and put the plum into a
cupboard and locked the door.

"I thought you didn't care about Christmas,"
said Jake.

"Well, I don't really. But it's the only time I get
candied plums. There's nothing in the world better
than a candied plum."

"Nothing?" asked Jake.

"Nothing," said Ben firmly.

"I bet there is," said Jake.

"Never," said Ben.

"I'll tell you what," said Jake. "I bet you I can find
three people who don't think a candied plum is the
best thing in the world."

"Tonight?" said Ben.

"Yes."

"What if I lose?" asked Ben.

"Then you give me the plum."

"No. I'd rather go to sleep," said Ben.

"But you *can't* sleep," said Jake.

Ben looked at his bed. The pillows were twisted. The sheets were tangled.
"All right," he agreed. "But what if I win? You're poor.
You've got nothing to give me."
"Then I'll help you to sleep," said Jake.
"Can you do that?"
"Oh, yes," said Jake.
And Ben thought he could.
"All right, then," he said.

So Ben wrapped up warm, took his candied plum,
and they set off. Jake led Ben down a long
alleyway, across a cobbled yard, and down
a short flight of stone steps.

There, beneath a big house, in a damp and dark cellar, was a Christmas party. The little mice were thin and poor. Their clothes were ragged, like Jake's, and the table was spread with only a poor feast. But the little mice scampered round and danced and squeaked with joy.

At last, one little mouse, worn
out with fun, sat against the wall.

"Here's your first test," said Jake. "Go on, now. Tell him you will give
him the plum if he'll leave the party and spend Christmas on his own."
Ben tried. The little mouse looked longingly at the plum.

"I'd love a candied plum," he said.

"It's yours," said Ben.

"I'll share it with the others," said the little mouse.

"No," said Jake. "You must leave the party and sit all alone and eat it all
yourself."

"I'd *love* a plum," said the little mouse.

"Take it," said Ben.

"No," he said. "I'll stay here. I'd rather be with the others, even without the
plum." And he scurried away and joined in the dancing.

"Let's go," said Jake. And Ben followed him, but not without a glance over
his shoulder at the children and a strange feeling in his heart.

Jake took Ben to an old inn.
The ceilings were low and the
beams were black, and the fire
burned brightly in the hearth.

A Christmas crowd of mice raised their glasses and drank a toast.
"To Christmas!"
Ben wished he had a glass to raise, and he took a nibble at his plum.
"Careful," warned Jake. "It will all be gone."
Ben wrapped the plum up in his scarf, to stop himself from nibbling it.
Jake took a glass, raised it in the air and said, "To Ben!"
But the other mice put their glasses down.
"I won't drink to him," said the oldest mouse.
"It would spoil Christmas."

Jake looked sad, and drank alone.
Ben's eyes filled with tears.
"Offer him the plum," said Jake.

Ben crept over and whispered in the old mouse's ear.
"Do you like candied plums?"
"I love them."
"If I give you this one, will you drink a health to Ben?"
The old mouse peered at Ben through cloudy eyes and
did not recognize him.
"No, I won't," he said. "It would spoil Christmas to
drink a health to that mean mouse."
"Let's go," said Jake. And he took
Ben gently by the arm.

They crossed back over the cobbled yard to Ben's house.

"You said *three* people," said Ben, clutching his candied plum.
"So I win. Help me to get to sleep."
"Are you tired then?" asked Jake.
"I want to go to sleep," said Ben.
They scurried across the big room. The fire was sleeping, warm in the grate. The tree was
holding its branches over their heads. The parcels lay ready for the morning. Ben twitched his
whiskers in greedy excitement.
Behind the wall, in the dark tunnels where the cats couldn't stalk and the dogs couldn't run,
Jake led Ben back.
"Not that way," said Ben. But Jake led him on, to Tim's room.

"I've never been in here," said Ben.

Tim lay in bed. A little parcel tied with a red ribbon end lay by his side on the floor. The grate was cold and empty. "Is he asleep?" said Ben. "You'll wake him."

"No, I won't," said Jake.

Ben edged towards the bed. "Is he all right?"

Jake looked solemn. Ben touched Tim's shoulder. "He's cold," he said. "And so thin."

"Yes," said Jake. "He's always cold."

"Is he all right?" Tim had not moved. Ben shook him.

"Look in the parcel," said Jake. "It's for you."

"But Tim's . . ."

"Look in the parcel."

Ben picked it up and read the label – "To Ben. Merry Christmas, from Tim."

He pulled the red ribbon end and opened the parcel.

"It's a grape," he said.

Ben reached out to shake Tim's shoulder again, but he let his hand fall before he touched him.

He looked round the cold, empty room, then he looked down at the thin, cold, still figure.

"Was it all he had?"

"Let's go back," said Jake. "I'll let you sleep."

"I'll leave him the plum," said Ben. And he left it at the foot of the bed.

"He won't want it now," said Jake. "Remember: I said three."

"Why?" asked Ben. "Why has it happened?"

"Remember the party," said Jake. "Remember the old mouse at the inn?"

"He wouldn't drink my health. He called me a mean mouse." Ben looked down again at Tim. "Is this my fault, then?"

Ben's room was warm and snug.
The embers glowed in the grate.
The covers were turned back. The
presents lay under the twig. Ben
snuggled down in bed.
"I won't sleep," he said.
"I really won't. Poor Tim. Isn't
there any way we can make him
all right? Is it too late?"
Jake pulled the covers up to Ben's
chin. Ben fell fast asleep.

Suddenly the bells were ringing. The
sun was gleaming bright and cold in
the frosty air. The icicles hung like
jewels in the light.

Ben jumped out of bed and fell over his candied plum.
He began to swear and shout and then stopped, put his
hand to his mouth and remembered.

He picked up the plum, ran down the tunnel, and burst into Tim's
room. Tim was lying quite still in his bed. The room was cold. As
the door banged open, he yawned, stretched, and said, "Merry
Christmas, Ben." Ben jumped in the air in his delight and nearly
knocked Tim out of bed as he hurled himself at the little mouse.
"Merry Christmas!" he shouted. And he flung the plum at him.
    "For me?"
        "Yes! And more! Lots more!"

Tim gave Ben the little parcel.
"It seems to have unwrapped itself
in the night," he said. "I'm sorry."
"I don't want it!" said Ben. "Keep it."
"It's your present," said Tim. "Please."
"It's the best grape in the world," said
Ben, without even looking in the parcel.
"Thank you. Come on."
He dragged Tim down the tunnel.

They bundled themselves up with the presents under the twig, and cheese and fruit
and wine and chocolates and more and more things until they could hardly walk.
Then Ben led Tim down the long alleyway, across the cobbled yard, down the
steps, and they burst into the party.

"Merry Christmas!" shouted Ben.

The mice looked surprised, and a little bit frightened when they saw Ben, but they cheered up when Tim peered over his shoulder.

"Merry Christmas!" they all called back.

And Ben spread his offerings on the table, and gave out his gifts, and shoveled all the coal on the fire at once and called out to the mice to run to his house and fill their buckets. So the room was hot and bright when the other mice arrived. And the dancing was fast. And the laughter was loud.

Ben saw the old mouse from the inn and thrust a glass into his hand. "Merry Christmas!" he said. And the old mouse drank. "To Ben!" said Tim. And they all called out, "To Ben!" And the old mouse hesitated. Then he raised his glass to his lips. When they were tired out, and the little ones were snoozing, and the older ones were blinking the sleep from their eyes, Ben and Tim went home, arm in arm.

They walked through the dark tunnel,
where the cats couldn't stalk and the dogs couldn't run.
"Merry Christmas," said Tim, and he turned toward his home. Ben said,
carefully, "Would you like to come over to my place?"